Not Ready For 10

CYNTHIA TAITT GUILLORY

Not Ready For 10

iUniverse books may be ordered through booksellers or by contacting:

iUniverse
1663 Liberty Drive
Bloomington, IN 47403
www.iuniverse.com
844-349-9409

Because of the dynamic nature of the Internet, any web addresses or links contained in this book may have changed since publication and may no longer be valid. The views expressed in this work are solely those of the author and do not necessarily reflect the views of the publisher, and the publisher hereby disclaims any responsibility for them.

Any people depicted in stock imagery provided by Getty Images are models, and such images are being used for illustrative purposes only.
Certain stock imagery © Getty Images.

ISBN: 978-1-5320-9985-4 (sc)
978-1-5320-9986-1 (e)

Library of Congress Control Number: 2020917004

Print information available on the last page.

iUniverse rev. date: 09/04/2020

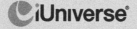

Not Ready For 10

In two short months, Nick will be 10! I'm not ready he says… can I be 9 again? Why, said his parents, would you want to be 9? Ten is really awesome you'll be just fine. No…said Nick and he shook his head…"Ten" means I have to stay in my own bed!

Well you are a big boy said Mama no need to fret! I will always check on you...now don't be upset. But what if I get lonely said Nick, or what if there's no light, what if I hear a noise that would give me a fright! Well, you have your friends Mickey, Hop, George and Oatmeal. I promise to tuck you in said Mama ...so do we have a deal?

Nick wasn't ready for a deal! He wasn't ready to try! He didn't want to be 10 and he started to cry. So, Mama and Dada held him in their arms they told him they loved him and would protect him from harm. They said a little prayer and when they were done. They went in together to tuck in their son. They both sat with him until he was asleep and then Mama and Dada left without a peep.

As Mama and Dada settled in to watch TV... in walked Nick who said…"I have to pee". Okay... then go on, said Mama then straight back to bed. So, off Nick went and he hung his head. Back in his room he heard many sounds, bumps, thumps, and creaks all around. He thought he saw a monster or was it a bat? He thought he saw an alien so straight up he sat. He wanted to turn the light on but was too afraid to move he needed Mama & Dada and didn't know what to do. Just as he was about to panic and was ready to scream in walked Mama out of nowhere it seemed. 'How are you doing Sugar?" "Do you need the light on?" "Are you okay?" "Should I sing you a song?"

Mama turned on the lights and together they checked the room. No monsters, no aliens, just toys and a balloon. Then all of a sudden, they heard a "THUMP" and quickly thereafter they heard a "BUMP"! That thump and that bump made both of them jump! Mama called out "Dada" is that you? Then Mama knew just what she had to do. The noise came from the attic and so she got up and then she saw Dada who had gotten kind of stuck.

But once he got free, he handed Mama a tiny little lamp. It was one he had used when he was a kid at camp. It was just enough light for Nick to feel safe. Mama knew just where to put it… she had just the place. She went into Nick's room put it by his bedside and Nick let out a tiny little sigh. He snuggled in his bed and settled down and soon his frown turned upside down. Then Mama tiptoed out of Nick's room and he slept all night by the light of the moon. When the morning came Nick bounced in...to Mama and Dada's room with a big ole grin! I did it! I did it! He said again and again! I think I am finally ready to turn 10!

MISSING IMAGE

<< INSERT FNL_06>>

*** END ***

CPSIA information can be obtained
at www.ICGtesting.com
Printed in the USA
LVHW070540160920
666130LV00002B/2

9 781532 099854